Is your Grandmother a Goanna?

Pamela Allen

Animals

withdrawn

For Thomas and Toby

PUFFIN BOOKS

Published by the Penguin Group
Penguin Group (Australia)
250 Camberwell Road
Camberwell, Victoria 3124, Australia
(a division of Pearson Australia Group Pty Ltd)
Penguin Group (USA) Inc.
375 Hudson Street, New York, New York 10014, USA
Penguin Group (Canada)
90 Eglinton Avenue East, Suite 700, Toronto ON M4P 2Y3, Canada
(a division of Pearson Penguin Canada Inc.)
Penguin Books Ltd
80 Strand, London WC2R 0RL, England
Penguin Ireland
25 St Stephen's Green, Dublin 2, Ireland
(a division of Penguin Books Ltd)
Penguin Books India Pvt Ltd
11, Community Centre, Panchsheel Park, New Delhi-110 017, India
Penguin Group (NZ)
67 Apollo Drive, Rosedale, North Shore 0632, New Zealand
(a division of Pearson New Zealand Ltd)
Penguin Books (South Africa) (Pty) Ltd
24 Sturdee Avenue, Rosebank, Johannesburg 2196, South Africa

Penguin Books Ltd, Registered Offices: 80 Strand, London WC2R 0RL, England

First published by Penguin Group (Australia), 2007
This paperback edition published by Penguin Group (Australia), 2009

10 9 8 7 6 5 4 3 2 1

Design by Deborah Brash © Penguin Group (Australia)
Typeset in 22pt Granjon
Printed in China by Everbest Printing Co Ltd

National Library of Australia
Cataloguing-in-Publication data:

Allen, Pamela.
Is your grandmother a goanna? / Pamela Allen.

ISBN: 978 0 14 350208 1

Grandparent and child – Juvenile fiction.

Animals – Juvenile fiction.

A823.3

puffin.com.au

One day a little boy set out to visit his grandmother.

He went to the railway station.
On the platform stood the station master.
'I'm going to visit my grandmother,'
said the little boy
and he climbed onto the train.

The station master blew his whistle,
Wheeeeeeeeeeee!
The train went Tooooo! Tooooo!
and off they went.

Chuffa Chuffa Chuffa Chuffa,
Chuffa Chuffa Chuffa Chuffa,
Chuffa Chuffa Chuffa Chuffa,

Chuffa Chuffa Chuffa Chuffa,
Chuffa Chuffa Chuffa Chuffa,
Faster Faster Faster Faster,

until they reached the next station.

On the platform stood the station master.
The little boy climbed down from the train.
'Have you seen my grandmother?' he asked.

'There are only elephants here,' replied the
station master. 'Is your grandmother an elephant?'

'No!' cried the little boy
and he climbed back onto the train.
The station master blew his whistle, Wheeeeeeeeeeee!
The train went Tooooo! Tooooo! and off they went.

Chuffa Chuffa Chuffa Chuffa,
Chuffa Chuffa Chuffa Chuffa,
Chuffa Chuffa Chuffa Chuffa,

Chuffa Chuffa Chuffa Chuffa,
Chuffa Chuffa Chuffa Chuffa,
Faster Faster Faster Faster,

until they reached the next station.

On the platform stood the station master.
The little boy climbed down from the train.
'Have you seen my grandmother?' he asked.

'There are only walruses here,' replied the
station master. 'Is your grandmother a walrus?'

'No!' cried the little boy
and he climbed back onto the train.
The station master blew his whistle, Wheeeeeeeeeeee!
The train went Tooooo! Tooooo! and off they went.

Chuffa Chuffa Chuffa Chuffa,
Chuffa Chuffa Chuffa Chuffa,
Chuffa Chuffa Chuffa Chuffa,

Chuffa Chuffa Chuffa Chuffa,
Chuffa Chuffa Chuffa Chuffa,
Faster Faster Faster Faster,

until they reached the next station.

On the platform stood the station master.
The little boy climbed down from the train.
'Have you seen my grandmother?' he asked.

'There are only goannas here,' replied the
station master. 'Is your grandmother a goanna?'

'No!' cried the little boy
and he climbed back onto the train.
The station master blew his whistle, Wheeeeeeeeeeee!
The train went Tooooo! Tooooo! and off they went.

Chuffa Chuffa Chuffa Chuffa,
Chuffa Chuffa Chuffa Chuffa,
Chuffa Chuffa Chuffa Chuffa,

Chuffa Chuffa Chuffa Chuffa,
Chuffa Chuffa Chuffa Chuffa,
Faster Faster Faster Faster,

until they reached the next station.

On the platform stood the station master.
The little boy climbed down from the train.
'Have you seen my grandmother?' he asked.

'There are only gorillas here,' replied the
station master. 'Is your grandmother a gorilla?'

'No!' cried the little boy
and he climbed back onto the train.
The station master blew his whistle, Wheeeeeeeeeeeee!
The train went Tooooo! Tooooo! and off they went.

Chuffa Chuffa Chuffa Chuffa,
Chuffa Chuffa Chuffa Chuffa,
Chuffa Chuffa Chuffa Chuffa,

Chuffa Chuffa Chuffa Chuffa,
Chuffa Chuffa Chuffa Chuffa,
Faster Faster Faster Faster,

until they reached the next station.

On the platform stood the station master.
The little boy climbed down from the train.
'Have you seen my grandmother?' he asked.

'There are only hippopotamuses here,' replied the
station master. 'Is your grandmother a hippopotamus?'

'No!' cried the little boy
and he climbed back onto the train.
The station master blew his whistle, Wheeeeeeeeeeee!
The train went Tooooo! Tooooo! and off they went.

Chuffa Chuffa Chuffa Chuffa,
Chuffa Chuffa Chuffa Chuffa,
Chuffa Chuffa Chuffa Chuffa,

Chuffa Chuffa Chuffa Chuffa,
Chuffa Chuffa Chuffa Chuffa,
Faster Faster Faster Faster,

until they reached the next station.

On the platform stood the station master.
The little boy climbed down from the train.
'Have you seen my grandmother?' he asked.

'Does she have grey wispy hair and a happy smile?'
asked the station master.

'Yes!' cried the little boy.
And there she was.
They hugged and hugged.
The station master blew his whistle, Wheeeeeeeeeeee!
The train went Tooooo! Tooooo! and off it went.

Chuffa Chuffa Chuffa Chuffa,
Chuffa Chuffa Chuffa Chuffa,
Chuffa Chuffa Chuffa Chuffa,

Chuffa Chuffa Chuffa Chuffa,
Chuffa Chuffa Chuffa Chuffa,
Faster Faster Faster Faster,

until it was right out of sight.

Chuffa Chuffa Chuffa Chuffa,
Chuffa Chuffa Chuffa Chuffa,
Chuffa Chuffa Chuffa Chuffa,
Chuffa Chuffa Chuffa Chuffa,
Chuffa Chuffa Chuffa Chuffa.